20 BIG TRUCKS

in the Middle of Christmas

MARK LEE   illustrated by KURT CYRUS

CANDLEWICK PRESS

One doughnut truck, on a cold winter day,
drives into town and parks and stays.

It's Christmastime, so don't be late!
We watch and shiver as we wait.
Snow in the mountains. Ice on the roads.
We'll need big trucks to bring big loads.

A snowplow and sander are trucks two and three.

And truck number four brings our evergreen tree.

Truck five is a digger with a big earth drill
that cuts a hole into the ground.

Six is a crane that lifts our tree high
and ever so carefully brings it down.

Honk! Honk! Make way
for trucks seven, eight, nine,
with silver flakes and golden bells
and strings of lights that shine.

Our Christmas tree is green and tall.
String the lights—just please don't fall!
A hook and ladder, but there's no fire.
Truck ten helps them reach much higher.

We count each truck
and say their names.
Boom truck eleven has
a basket crane.

A stake truck carries a holiday band,

three elves, and a dancing snowman.

Thirteen, fourteen, fifteen bring
a Christmas village built for fun.

Sixteen pulls a generator.

Switch it on to make things run!

The choir van broke down—won't go!
But tow truck seventeen saves the show.

A flatbed carries Santa's sleigh.
All eighteen trucks, please go this way!

Count kids and dads and babies and mamas
and truck nineteen with Christmas llamas.

Now raise the star.
Up . . . up . . .

then down!
And with a crash, it hits
the ground.

No star to top our Christmas tree?
Will they listen? Can they see?

"Stop! Look! Hear our plan!"
"Could we?"
"Should we?"
"Yes, we can!"

The doughnut is wrapped with red and green lights.
The power clicks on and our tree glows bright.

One last truck. No time to pause.
A pickup truck brings Santa Claus!

Now friends and families sing and witness
twenty big trucks in the middle of Christmas!
Have a doughnut, please. Hot chocolate, too.
Merry Christmas to mamas and llamas—and you!

For MK—who loves Christmas

ML

First edition 2021

Library of Congress Catalog Card Number pending
ISBN 978-1-5362-1253-2

21 22 23 24 25 26 CCP 10 9 8 7 6 5 4 3 2 1

Printed in Shenzhen, Guangdong, China

This book was typeset in New Century Schoolbook.

Candlewick Press
99 Dover Street
Somerville, Massachusetts 02144

www.candlewick.com